Series 401
A Ladybird Book

*FIVE LITTLE KITTENS is a delightfully
exciting story told in verse, which not only
reveals a 'chapter of accidents' when
Mummy goes out shopping, but also a
happy ending when she returns . . . and
the story is charmingly illustrated with
24 coloured pictures.*

FIVE LITTLE KITTENS

Story and illustrations by   A. J. MACGREGOR

Verses by   W. PERRING

Publishers: Ladybird Books Ltd . Loughborough
© Ladybird Books Ltd (formerly Wills & Hepworth Ltd) 1955
Printed in England

Mrs. Tibbets, going shopping,
　　Wasn't pleased enough to purr;
" Kitties, PLEASE ! " she said quite crossly,
　　" How can Mummy brush her fur ? "

But the frisky little kittens
　　Didn't think of that at all :
Mopsie said she'd like a trumpet,
　　Muffie asked her for a ball.

Patch kept on and on—" An engine ! "
　　Ginger said, " I'd like a flag ! "
Snowball's mind was full of motors :
　　Mummy said : " Now, where's my bag ? "

0 7214 0213 5

Off she set, with her umbrella,

— For it had begun to rain—

Said : " Now *please* be good, you kitties!

'Till I get back home again."

So she waited on the corner,

In the rain, to catch the bus.

Kitties waved, and "Well!" said Mopsie,

"Fancy saying that to US!"

" We will show how good we can be;
　　She will not believe her eyes!
If we finish all the cleaning,
　　Won't it be a grand surprise? "

So she put on Mummy's apron,
　　Which was hanging by the sink :—
" Everybody must do something,
　　I will wash the pots . . . I think ! "

Snowball took the brush and dustpan,

    Patch said he would have the broom;

Ginger took the mop and bucket

    Up the stairs to clean their room.

Muffie said she'd clear the breakfast,

    Patch said: " I'll sweep up ! " and then

Mopsie said : " Now, everybody

    Must be done by half past ten ! "

Snowball, busy on the staircase,

   Thought it was as good as play,

Never gave a thought to Muffie

   Packing pots up on the tray.

Muffie, with her tray full-loaded,

Slowly came across the hall.

—(Careful, now!)—no thought of Snowball

Crossed her busy mind at all.

Mopsie, working in the kitchen,

Heard a sudden fearful crash,

Sounds of breaking cups and saucers

Thought : '' Oh, goodness, what a
smash ! ''

Rushed to find out what had happened,

   Towards the woeful waiting scene;

" Oh ! " she cried, and " Bless my whiskers !

   What an accident there's been ! "

Then she tripped upon her apron,

Fell full-length into the hall,

Strewed with broken cups and saucers,

Oh, great Catkins! What a fall!

On the scene came Patch and Ginger,

Gazed upon the littered floor.

Shattered pots and scattered kittens,

Sad, and sorrowful—and sore!

Then with mop and brush and dustpan

They began to sweep it up;

Every scrap of splintered saucer

Every chip of broken cup!

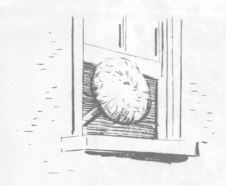

Ginger saw his mop was dirty,

    Said : " I think it needs a shake."

Poked it through the open window,

    —But it was a *sad* mistake.

For it struck a large policeman

    Who was passing down the street—

" Ow ! " he cried, " Insulting conduct

    To a policeman on his beat ! "

P.C. Bobs was *very* angry,
    And his face was quite severe,
As he looked in through the window,
    Ginger thought, " Oh dear ! oh DEAR ! "

And he thought, " Well, now I've done it ! "
    And he didn't know what to say :
Thought : " I know he'll not believe me ! "
    And began to run away !

In went Bobby, through the window:

Just then Mummy came along,

Saw the feet go through with horror,

Thought, " There's something *very*
wrong ! "

Seized a foot and pulled and pulled it,

    P.C. Bobs let out a roar;

" Out you come ! " said Mrs. Tibbets,

    " Honest folk go through the door ! "

Then she saw it was a policeman,

    Not a thief, that she had caught.

And was quite relieved on finding

    He was not what she had thought.

" Why, Mr. Bobs ! " said Mrs. Tibbets,

 —For she knew him very well—

" What is wrong ? What are you doing ? "

 What a tale he had to tell !

At the door, the kittens met them,
    Solemn-eyed, a silent group:
First was Ginger, very sheepish,
    Then a tearful timid troop.

" Well, indeed ! " said Mrs. Tibbets,
    " There's a naughty trick to play ! "
Ginger bit his claws, and wondered
    What could *any* kitten say?

" Please," he mumbled, "please, I'm sorry !

    Very sorry, Mr. Bobs !

We were only helping Mummy,

    Doing all the cleaning jobs !

And I didn't mean to hit you ! "

    —Ginger very nearly cried !

" That's all right ! " said Bobby, grinning,

    " But you *should* have looked outside ! "

Off he went, and Mrs. Tibbets
    Went inside—Oh, what a shock,
When she saw the broken china,
    What a frightened little flock!

But she wasn't *very* angry
    When she saw how hard they'd tried,
Saw their sorry little faces
    (Patch and Muffie even cried.)

"Never mind, my dears!" she told them,

As they gathered round the chair.

Then she opened up her basket:

Didn't all the kittens stare!

Muffie's ball ! . . . and Mopsie's trumpet !

   Snowball's motor ! . . . Ginger's flag !

Yes, and there was Patch's engine !

   All were there in Mummy's bag !

How those happy kittens scampered !

   . . . There is little more to tell :

All their troubles now were over,

   All was well that ended well !